The Crimson Balloons

Know your deeper secrets

Riddhima Sen

Ukiyoto Publishing

All global publishing rights are held by

Ukiyoto Publishing

Published in 2022

Content Copyright © Riddhima Sen

ISBN 9789360167899

*All rights reserved.
No part of this publication may be reproduced, transmitted, or stored in a retrieval system, in any form by any means, electronic, mechanical, photocopying, recording or otherwise, without the prior permission of the publisher.*

The moral rights of the authors have been asserted.

*This is a work of fiction. Names, characters, businesses, places, events, locales, and incidents are either the products of the author's imagination or used in a fictitious manner. Any resemblance to actual persons, living or dead, or actual events is purely coincidental.
This book is sold subject to the condition that it shall not by way of trade or otherwise, be lent, resold, hired out or otherwise circulated, without the publisher's prior consent, in any form of binding or cover other than that in which it is published.*

Acknowledgement

I would like to express my gratitude towards Ukiyoto Publishing House for providing me with this golden opportunity.

Contents

Chapter 1: The Crimson Ballons	1
Chapter 2: Journal Entry	2
Chapter 3: Shrivelled petails of roses	3
Chapter 4: Conversation	4
Chapter 5: The Vessel of life	5
Chapter 6: Micro tale	6
Chapter 7: Flannels of elegance	7
Chapter 8: Bloody Snowflakes Short Story	8
Chapter 9: Companions Forever	11
Chapter 10: Kiosks of Delusion	12
Chapter 11: Inked Ballons	13
Chapter 12: Indigo Waves	14
Chapter 13: Stairway to heaven	15
Chapter 14: Innovation marketing and technology	16
Chapter 15: Shades of happy moments	17
Chapter 16: Snowy mountains	18
Chapter 17	19

The Flashback	*19*
Chapter 18	21
The Revelation	*21*
Chapter 19	22
A poet who became a criminal, but why?	*22*
Chapter 20	24
Continuation	*24*
About the Author	*25*

Chapter 18

The Revelation

Approximately two hours later, the police reached the hotel room. Anthony's corpse lay on the floor, caked in blood. The letter revealed that Anthony was actually an illegal immigrant who had fled to Siberia, and murdered the family of the real Anthony. According to the police, it was a suicide case. But, who knew it was a murder, committed by an abstract thing – guilt?

The diary read:

Chapter 19

A poet who became a criminal, but why?

Faded Dandelions
My love, do you still remember
The days of explicit bliss;
When we were companions,
Bosom companions who could never be separated.
Lovers for an eternal timespan,

I still remember,
The warm smell of your blue cotton t-shirt,
The comfortable space in the lawn
Where we used to talk our hearts out,
Now, you have abandoned me
We may never be united again,
But, the memory of the sultry evening
Clinging to the fabric of your nylon cardigan

My pink sweater,

Continues to be persistent

Down my memory lane

The elegant view of the cherry blossoms

Strewn in my heart,

Light pinkish speckles

On my bleeding heart,

People go away,

But memories remain.

Although my heartstrings are baked with blood,

And embellished with the innards of my faint heart

I still cherish the memories of La Amour.

The dandelions have faded, beloved

White and shrunken.

Chapter 20

Continuation

The shades of insanity

How can we describe insanity ?
Maybe a   condition of   mental unstability   ,
Where a person is retarded mentally
Devoid of the capacity to think normally
But,
Is that really the definition of insanity?

The hustles and bustles of daily life
Filled with excessive workload,
Hypertension,
And a pile of deadlines
And assignments and files
Isn't that insanity   ,
Of modern issues
And lifestyle?

Chapter 1: The Crimson Ballons

What are the ingredients of a perfect evening

1)A bosom friend

2) An eloquent scenery

3) A silent beach

And

4) A Vibrant Sky

Chapter 2: Journal Entry

Wonderful, lustrous garments
Woven with numerous colourful threads,
Tints of bright scarlet,
Mountain blue, the representative of tranquillity;
And pastel shades, subtle yet pretty.

About the Author

Riddhima Sen

Riddhima Sen is currently studying at Jadavpur University, Kolkata, Comparative Literature, ug1. She is an introvert who likes to read books and write poetry. She even likes to design garments and exciting apparel. She is a Social Media Intern at Younity, a volunteer at Hamari Pahchan NGO, a curriculum writing intern at Team Everest, and the Vice President of the Architecture Club, SUPROS. She desires to enjoy life to the fullest and wants to try every activity under the sun. She likes to recite poems and compose lyrics as well. By participating in leadership programs, she has overcome her introversion to a great extent.

www.ingramcontent.com/pod-product-compliance
Lightning Source LLC
LaVergne TN
LVHW041643070526
838199LV00053B/3527

Chapter 3: Shrivelled petails of roses

Strewn all along the path,

Chrome yellow with the dust of life,

Coated with mendacity,

Monotonous shades of dull grey

Tinted with speckles of black

Which represent life,

In its rawest self;

Embedded in darkening shapes

Leaning against the sidewalk

Life is just a rollercoaster ride, truly.

Chapter 4: Conversation

Lily: Hey, Cactus, how are you doing?

Cactus: Hey, I'm good. What about you?

Lily: Yeah, I am hale and hearty as ever, what can even go wrong with me when I'm so white and pure. You are so rough and unsophisticated.

Cactus: I am not ugly, your thoughts are ugly and filthy.

Chapter 5: The Vessel of life

Man : What is the meaning of life?

Philosopher : Well , it's an individual's journey from the starting point to the ending point .

Man : If life is so miserable, and full of challenges, why should we live it ?

Philosopher: Because the vessel of life crosses the river of faith , compassion, kindness and positivity atleast once , it does not always face tempestuous winds which cause the seas to shriek, and emit salty tears in the form of waves . The vessel of life is crafted with rosewood and redwood , at the same time . It's a journey worth embarking upon , even though it's an amalgamation of happiness and sadness.

Chapter 6: Micro tale

The irony of the society

Once there was an old man, who was ailing and lying on the streets, absolutely helpless. People looked at him, but no one dared to help him until the poor soul finally succumbed to the illness and was no longer a member of the two-faced hypocrisy.

Chapter 7: Flannels of elegance

Vibrant hues,

Glittering through the abyss of darkness;

Like an insignia of human will

Which emerges victorious at the end of a tedious and bloody battle,

Bathed in blood, red and radiant,

Will finally shine in the violet horizon, painted with a thousand shades

Flannels of elegance,

Painted in mountain blue and silver

Celebrate the victor's song.

Chapter 8: Bloody Snowflakes Short Story

May 2000. The morning sun shone radiantly across the horizon. It was a warm, sunlit morning in the city of Chicago. Sam, a software engineer at a multinational company, Blue Ways, was sitting on the porch of his apartment. There was a blue coffee cup on the porcelain table. An ashtray filled with burnt cigarettes lay beside the cup. It was around 10 a.m. in the morning. The lush green porch shone bright green in the dazzling sunlight, devoid of any particular hue. A book titled "A Yellow Sky" was in his hands. Sam was deeply engrossed while reading the book. It was a tale of deep, engraved sorrow. The story of an orphan teenager, who fought against the crude society to fulfill his dream of becoming a cricketer, in the snowy land of Alaska.

Sam could resonate with the poor boy's struggle for sustenaince. He himself was an orphan. He aspired to become a renowned radio jockey since the age of 11. A young and loving couple had adopted him 11 years ago, from an orphanage in Chicago. They were more than his own parents to him since they showered tremendous love on him. Currently, he was one of the top radio jockeys at Blue Moon FM Studio. Although it was a part-time job, he enjoyed his work. He lived all alone, and his adoptive parents had passed away in an accident, over a year ago. When he reached the thirty-fourth page of the book, suddenly the doorbell rang. He proceeded to open the door and stared at the gigantic grandfather clock on the eastern wall. A young boy, around 11 years old, stood outside the door. He was clad in tattered clothes, and told him "Do you want to buy some snacks?" The boy seemed identical to the protagonist of the story. Even he used to sell warm snacks in the cold neighbourhood.

Sam took some burgers and paid him ten dollars. The boy left immediately. He returned to the spacious patio consequently. The bright afternoon sun shone radiantly across the red horizon, it was 1 pm the day. After devouring a sumptuous lunch comprising bacon, peas, potatoes, and warm chicken soup, he fell asleep on the couch. Abruptly, he found himself inside the story. It was Timmy, the protagonist of the story by Robert White, a renowned author. He was travelling across the snow-laden paths and crossroads when he stumbled across a mob chasing a rebel. He was hit by a bullet all of a sudden.

The next day, Sam was found dead by the police on his couch, caked with blood, and a pistol lay at his side. His blood had splattered on the snow inside a glass globe, which had broken into pieces, completely shattered into million pieces. No one knew how he passed away, despite the anti-depressant pills found in his chamber. Maybe, it was telepathy, who knows.

Chapter 9: Companions Forever

Friends are like a

colorful rainbow,

Amid the abyss of mendacity;

Like splashes of violet and blue,

And color patches of blue and mountain silver,

Are the insignia of life, truly

Glittering in the horizon,

Friends are the light of life.

Chapter 10: Kiosks of Delusion

Kiosks of delusion,

Floating in the air like red wine;

Full of fake hopes and dreams

Clogging the pensive mind

Chapter 11: Inked Ballons

Balloons of thought,

Afloat in the sky;

Tinged with vibrant tints

Of dark blue, and bright yellow

Are inked on milky white sheets of paper,

As dreams.

Inked dreams are made of colorful thoughts,

Embellished with imagination

And pearls of happiness,

Inked dreams represent a poet's inner thoughts.

Chapter 12: Indigo Waves

Indigo waves,

Spread across the horizon;

In fragments,

When we were free for the first time,

The day when we tasted freedom for the very first time,

On 15th August 1947;

The British Rule finally got distinguished,

At the stroke of midnight;

It seemed as if an ocean had been conjured,

With the smiles and exuberance of the "freedmen",

And the tiranga

Flying in the azure sky.

Chapter 13: Stairway to heaven

Stairway to heaven,
Shrewn with petals of roses;
And a divine elegance
Brightening up the way.

As lustrous and illuminated as the starry night,
Studded with diamond-like pieces of the cosmos,
White and offwhite in hue;
A staircase carved out of planetoids,
And gateways carved of asteroids,
Lead to the land of Eden,
The city of the Almighty,
Equivalent to Olympus in Greek mythology.

Chapter 14: Innovation marketing and technology

Innovation marketing is a method of promoting new products and services in the process of innovation. It is definitely a modern type of marketing. For example, in the case of a new product, innovation marketing is really important for innovative products. Technology is the application of scientific knowledge to the practical aims of human life or, as it is sometimes phrased, to the change and manipulation of the human environment. For example, an automatic car is a form of innovation. There is an interrelated web between innovation marketing and technology. Now, innovation marketing involves b2b and b2c as well.

Chapter 15: Shades of happy moments

Those exuberant moments spent with grandparents,

The childhood moments shared with them

Are unparalleled;

The smell of the old woven sweaters

Is still as fresh as the time it was woven.

Like a bright kaleidoscope,

Bathed in red, yellow, and orange lights

Those photographic memories will be cherished in my heart forever.

Those fairy tales and rounds of ludo played

Will be forever etched in my heart in golden letters.

Chapter 16: Snowy mountains

The iced mountain caps

It was already 7 am in morning, and Anthony had woken up in the morning. He looked outside the enormous hotel window and glanced at the white, snowy landscape. The entire city seemed to be wrapped in a white blanket, as white as milk and as soft as the clouds afloat in the sky.

The sultry winter morning of December in Siberia had been a difficult one. Anthony was a twenty-year old man, who owned a chocolate shop in a city near the outskirts of Siberia. He was escaping from a group of gangsters, who had murdered his entire family. His diary, "The Crimson Balloons" lay on the table. The diary was of a dark reddish hue. Surprisingly, there was a poem based on India there. He himself didn't know how he wrote it. But, he did receive a letter from a random Indian person, when things were normal. The gangsters had planned to assassinate him as well, because of a century-old rivalry. He was of Siberian origin , and it was really astonishing for him . A few months ago , his parents were murdered brutally .

Chapter 17

The Flashback

Two months ago, Sam and his gang members started following him. He had to leave his shop and flee. All of a sudden, he found a letter in the diary. When he read it, he was shocked beyond apprehension, all of a sudden, as fast as a flash of lightning a gunshot was heard. The diary was wide open, and a poem read –

<u>Steps to Heavenly Love</u>

Divinity is something that exists in their realm,

The Garden in East Eden;

Where primordial love blossoms between two individuals,

Maybe it was a sin,

According to the Almighty

And the couple was banished from Eden.

Love is not a sin,

Unlike the seven sins mentioned in the Bible,

And it is absolutely humane to immerse deep in the sea of love,

As wide as the horizon,

Where the reddish-orange sun sets against the elegant pink sky,

As eloquent as a painting,

Even though the event was a conspiracy,

It led to the creation of the human race.